CW00969542

Gumdrop

on the Farm

Val Biro

Published by the Penguin Group
Penguin Books Ltd, 27 Wrights Lane, London
W8 5TZ, England
Penguin Books Australia Ltd, Ringwood,
Victoria, Australia
Penguin Books Canada Ltd, 10 Alcorn Avenue,
Toronto, Ontario, Canada M4V 3B2
Penguin Books (NZ) Ltd, 182-190 Wairau Road,
Auckland 10, New Zealand

Penguin Books Ltd, Registered Offices:
Harmondsworth, Middlesex, England

This edition first published in Great Britain in 1984
by Hodder and Stoughton

This edition published by Claremont Books,
an imprint of Godfrey Cave Associates Limited,
42 Bloomsbury Street, London, WC1B 3QJ,
under licence from Val Biro, 1996

Copyright © 1984 Val Biro

ISBN 1 854 71794 4

It was a fine summer and Mr Oldcastle was on a farm holiday. In a field near the farm he set up a blue tent for himself, a small red tent for his dog Horace, and a large yellow tent for his vintage car Gumdrop.

They were all very snug and comfortable.

One day Farmer Hearn came across the field. 'My tractor has broken down,' he said, 'and I wonder if you would help me get the hay in with your car?'

So Gumdrop spent the whole day carting hay. He pulled a trailer full of bales, and there was hay piled up on his back seat too. It was hard work, but all the bales were safely in by night.

Next morning Mr Oldcastle was ready for a good breakfast, but he had run out of eggs.

'Come on, Horace,' he called, 'let's fetch some in Gumdrop.'

He opened the back door for the dog, but there, lo and behold, they found two hens sitting comfortably on a pile of hay!

One thing Horace likes doing best is to chase after hens. He is a very naughty dog. So he leapt into Gumdrop with such barks and yelps that the hens jumped out of the other side with the most terrible squawks and screeches.

'Come back, Horace!' yelled Mr Oldcastle, but it was no good. The dog took no notice and he was away, chasing the hens.

A donkey was munching some thistles
under a tree, but all that barking and
squawking made him jump. When he saw
the dog and the hens he thought they
were after him.
So he kicked out and ran away, bellowing
and braying dismally as he went.

Some piglets were having breakfast at a trough. All that braying and bellowing made them look up in alarm. When they saw a dangerous donkey galloping towards them, they promptly scampered away as fast as their fat little legs would carry them.
And how they squealed!

This was too much for Mr Oldcastle. His dog was chasing all the farm animals right out into the wood! What would Farmer Hearn say?

There was only one thing to do. He jumped into Gumdrop and drove after Horace. 'Come back, you horrible hound!' he shouted at his disobedient animal. Gumdrop gathered speed and joined the chase.

Up in the woods a fox was hiding under a bush. He was hungry because he had had no breakfast yet. He was always hungry. So he pricked up his ears when he heard those squeals.

'Here comes my breakfast!' he said, and leapt out of the bush to get those piglets.

A hungry fox is a dangerous animal.
When the piglets saw him they promptly
turned tail and scampered back,
squealing even louder.
The donkey had no wish to collide with
squealing piglets, so he wheeled round
and galloped back the way he came.
The hens were so alarmed by those
trampling hooves that they took wing and
flew into the air.
That left Horace who saw a hungry fox
bounding towards him.

Here was something even better to chase! Horace sprang forward. The fox was frightened at the sight of a barking dog, especially as it was closely followed by a honking vintage car.

'Catch him, Horace! Good boy!' urged Mr Oldcastle as dog and car pursued him back to the wood. But the fox was too quick for them and he soon got away.

The farm animals were safe. The piglets were back at the trough finishing their breakfast, the donkey continued munching his thistles under the tree and the hens were scratching peacefully near their henhouse. When Gumdrop and Horace returned from their fox hunt all was well again.

Except that there were still no eggs for breakfast.

Horace was sitting on the back seat and suddenly he barked twice. Mr Oldcastle looked. There beside the dog, lo and behold, he saw two new-laid eggs on a pile of hay!

Level 4 is ideal for ch
longer stories with a wic
to start reading indeper

Special features:

Clear type

Full, exciting story

Richer, more varied vocabulary

Once upon a time, there was a boy called Dick Whittington. He didn't have any parents, and he didn't have any money.

One day Dick said, "I'm going to London to look for work."

LONDON

6

7

Longer sentences

Detailed illustrations to capture the imagination

London was a long way away and Dick walked for days and days. When he got there, it was not at all like his home.

Educational Consultant: Geraldine Taylor

Book Banding Consultant: Kate Ruttle

LADYBIRD BOOKS

UK | USA | Canada | Ireland | Australia
India | New Zealand | South Africa

Ladybird Books is part of the Penguin Random House group of companies
whose addresses can be found at global.penguinrandomhouse.com.

ladybird.com

Penguin
Random House
UK

First published 2015
005

Printed in China

A CIP catalogue record for this book is available from the British Library

ISBN: 978-0-723-28066-8

Dick Whittington

Illustrated by Victoria Assanelli

Once upon a time, there was a boy called Dick Whittington. He didn't have any parents, and he didn't have any money.

One day Dick said, "I'm going to London to look for work."

LONDON →

7

London was a long way away
and Dick walked for days and
days. When he got there, it was
not at all like his home.

In London there were lots of big houses and lots of shops.

"There must be work for me here," Dick said. So he asked for work in all the big houses and all the shops, but there was nothing for him.

11

Dick had nowhere to go. He was so tired that he went to sleep on the doorstep of a big house.

A cook came out of the door and said, "You can't sleep here! Go away at once."

Just then, the man who lived in the house came home. He was called Mr Fitzwarren, and he was very rich.

"This boy has nowhere to go," he said to the cook. "He can work in the kitchen."

So Dick worked hard in the kitchen every day.

Mr Fitzwarren was very pleased and gave him some money.

At night, Dick slept in a room at the top of the house. The room was just big enough for his bed.

But every night, as Dick tried to sleep, rats and mice jumped about on his bed.

"A cat would catch all these rats and mice," said Dick. "I must go and buy a cat."

The next day, Dick saw a woman who had a beautiful cat to sell.

"Can this cat catch rats and mice?" asked Dick.

"This cat is the best rat and mouse catcher in London," said the woman.

"Then I would like to buy her," said Dick.

Dick gave the woman his money.
He took the cat home.

When he went to bed that night,
the cat chased the rats and mice
away. At last, Dick had a good
night's sleep.

Mr Fitzwarren had a beautiful daughter called Alice. Alice wanted to help Dick.

"My father has lots of ships," she said. "He sells goods to rich people in countries far away. Give him something to sell, and then you can be rich."

"What can I sell?" said Dick.
"All I have is my cat."

"Then my father will take your cat and sell it," said Alice.

Dick did not want to sell his cat, but he wanted to please Alice.

27

Dick gave his cat to Mr Fitzwarren.

"This cat is the best rat and mouse catcher in London," said Dick. "Will you sell her for me?"

"Yes, I'll sell your cat for you, Dick," said Mr Fitzwarren.

Dick missed his cat. Every night, the rats and mice came back and jumped about on Dick's bed. This made Dick very unhappy.

"I don't like London," said Dick. "I'm going back home."

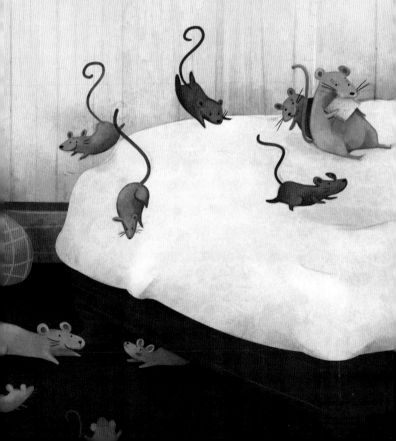

So the next day, Dick set out for home. Just as he was leaving London, he heard the church bells.

*"Turn again, Whittington,
Lord Mayor of London.*

*Turn again, Whittington,
three times mayor of London."*

"The bells are calling me back to London!" said Dick.

So Dick turned and went back
to Mr Fitzwarren's house.
When he got there, everyone
was sleeping. No one had seen
him leave.

Mr Fitzwarren's ship was sailing to a country far away. The king and queen of that country wanted to buy some goods.

As he was leaving on the ship to go and see them, Mr Fitzwarren took Dick's cat with him.

37

The king and queen had a beautiful palace, but there were mice and rats running all over it.

Mr Fitzwarren said, "I have a cat that can help you."

Dick's cat chased all the rats and mice away from the palace forever.

The king and queen wanted
to buy Dick's cat, but the cat
wanted to go home.

The king and queen said,
"This beautiful cat has helped us.
Take her home and give this
money to her master."

So Mr Fitzwarren took the cat
back to London.

When Mr Fitzwarren came home, he gave the money and the cat to Dick. Dick was pleased to have the money, and he was even more pleased to see his cat again.

The money made him rich, and not long after, he married Alice.

43

Dick, Alice and the cat lived
happily ever after.

And the people of London made
Dick their lord mayor three times,
just as the bells had said.

45

How much do you remember about the story of Dick Whittington? Answer these questions and find out!

- Where does Dick go to look for work?

- Why can't Dick sleep at night?

- What does Dick give to Mr Fitzwarren to sell?

- What does the cat do in the palace?

- What calls Dick back to London?

- How many times is Dick made lord mayor?